Dedicated to us everywhere

**Get inside the lives of
Jaka, Nina, Tashi and Sean.**

**Novel available
Fall 2015**

Inside Her

Akhaji Zakiya

Copyright © 2014 by Akhaji Zakiya

All rights reserved. No part of this work may be reproduced or utilized in any form or by any means without the written permission of the author.

This book is a work fiction. Names, characters, places, and incidents either are the products of the author's imagination or are used fictitiously, and any resemblance to actual persons, living or dead, locales is entirely coincidental.

Cover layout/design: Kim Quashie

ISBN 978-1-4997-6478-9

akhajizakiya.com
@akhajizakiya

For all the lovely souls who made this possible...

To Adrian without whom this project would not exist. Thanks for all the encouragement and editing help! Love you always.

To my parents for being there and sharing all that they could.

To Aunty Joyce a rock of steady truth, support and love.

To Maisha, Dianah, Tanisha, Lisa M., Tei, Chris, Kris, May and Linda C. for friendship and inspiration.

To Fiona Z. for *Bliss*, for being you and showing what is possible.

To Ahdri Z. for the beginnings.

Thanks also to Kim Q, all cover models, my friends and loves for listening, sharing feedback and stimulating my imagination.

Inside

inside me springs her
outside our expectation
oneness incited

Contents

Opening
  Jaka Meets Tashi, 3

Scenes from Novel
  1 Jaka - "Tall Chocolatte, Shaken…and Stirred", 11
  2 Nina - "And the Beat Goes On", 31
  3 Jaka & Nina - "Beyond", 55
  4 Sean - "Ready for the Weekend", 69

Tashi's Poems
  want love you, 85
  in this moment, 87
  Play Me, 89
  unexpectedly exciting (for Jaka), 91
  untitled, 93
  Used To Be, 95
  Recalibrate, 97
  on coming, 99
  revolutionary sounds, 101
  this lesbian poem, 103

Scenes from Novel

Opening
Jaka Meets Tashi

Jaka was having second thoughts about the whole thing.

'How smart was it to come all the way across town to this community cookout? By herself?' she questioned. 'Dragging Nina along would have been a much better idea.'

There she was, slightly overdressed in a white tank top and white fitted skirt which contrasted sharply against her coffee-bean skin. Feeling nervous about the unfamiliar, she smoothed her hand over the top of her short-haired head and took in the sights around her. Jaka was usually very comfortable in her agile, toned body – even when folks were beholding her on stage. But now, in a crowd of hundreds of gay people. Transgendered, bisexual, lesbian, queer people of all kinds. She was not sure she was in the right place.

It was a hot day. The cookout was on a long stretch of beach. Surrounded by dozens of big, colorful umbrellas pushed into the sand, people were in and out of the water...frolicking, playing beach volleyball, lounging, sipping and loving every minute of it. Most were of African, Asian and South Asian descent, many were chatting in lineups for BBQ and drinks. Everyone seemed excited to be there. Upbeat dance tunes with pulsating bass waved in the afternoon breeze. The sun blazed bodies and bounced off the water. Couples cuddled on large, beach towels. Muscle-chested men in tiny, tight swim trunks made friends and long-haired lesbians scoped out the scene behind tinted sunglasses.

It was overwhelming – the same-sex public displays of affection, the loud music, queer folks with strangely-coloured hair, tattoos and multiple piercings. It was especially overwhelming for Jaka who had never been to anything like this before. Well, not since the big street festivals that used to happen in her neighbourhood back in the day. Except those ones were not full of gay people...LBTQ people.

To get to the spot where she could see the beach and the festivities, Jaka had walked through a park. Its huge, thick-rooted, leafy trees provided shade to booths making up the community fair part of the cookout. Now, she wanted to go back to the shade. She was not sure she belonged here with all these folks. Not right now. She could, possibly, see herself freeing up and dancing a bit later if her kind of tunes came on. She was not ready yet.

As Jaka headed back to the comfortable shade of the park, she passed several booths and associated people. Beaming faces and bright-coloured marketing materials reflected messages from dozens of organizations and businesses – everything from breast cancer awareness to the annual Mr. Leather Bear contest to new products from banks and liquor companies. There was also a stage with performers and speakers announcing events relevant to the community. Jaka settled into the crook of one of the large, droopy willow trees and tried to ease into comfort.

Tashi first noticed Jaka while on stage announcing the upcoming human rights rally and encouraging people to sign the circulating petition. She tripped over her words momentarily when she glanced to the left and saw Jaka leaning up against a big tree. 'A true vision of loveliness,' Tashi thought to herself. 'How do I not know that sister?' She tried to make subtle eye contact to avoid being too obvious to onlookers, but Jaka's eyes were roaming the bustling crowd as if searching for something.

Realizing Jaka had not seen her yet, Tashi knew exactly where she would be heading when she left the stage. Causally of course, with her fist full of flyers providing a reason for an introduction. After repeating the rally date for the fourth time, she descended the stairs and could barely control her legs as they guided her. Causally still, Tashi floated toward the quiet radiance that called to her from that special willow tree. She felt compelled. Though she was not usually one to approach beautiful women she was not about to pass up this opportunity.

As she got closer, Tashi noticed that the subject of her interest was standing near Sean, a tennis instructor who had dated her ex's ex a couple of months ago.

'Leave it to Sean to always be around fineness,' she thought to herself. 'At least I can use that as an in…if need be.' Voices from the crowd blended into the background as Tashi swallowed hard and prepared to spread her message of freedom.

"Here's a flyer, hope you can come out next week," she said to the statuesque, long-eyelashed, muscled figure seeking shade under the bushy, sloped branches. The figure turned, hinted a smile and accepted the flyer. Shaking her head while reading, Jaka explained that she would not be able to make it. "Sounds interesting. I actually have a show that evening."

"Hey, that's cool," Tashi replied. "There will be more so I can keep you posted."

"Okay," Jaka sensed the come-on, but did not resist it. She was feeling more comfy now. Tashi, at a loss for words, yet wanting to keep the conversation going, said, "So, what show have you got going on?"

"A showcase at East Harbour High as part of an arts education project. I'm dancing with members of the company."

"The company?"

"Yeah, Rhythmnation."

"That's awesome! So you're a dancer dancer…like trained and everything. You know, I was wondering how you keep it so tight," Tashi blurted.

"Really?" Jaka inquired playfully. "How do you know I'm tight?" Her smile was deeper this time. She was feeling oddly at ease with this person. At least enough to flirt. Just a little bit. It is not often that an attractive girl, gay girl walks right up to her and says, 'Hi'.

"Um...I meant your muscles. The ones I can see...we can all see." Tashi stammered trying to recover. "Great physique."

Jaka looked up fully for the first time, directly into Tashi eyes. She said nothing. Filling the void, Tashi stated with all the cavalier confidence she could muster, "I'd like to see your beautiful self again. We should connect." As she slipped her phone out of her back pocket and unlocked it, Jaka deliberately took it out of her hand. Her eyes did not leave Tashi's face until she was ready to enter digits. When she was done, she handed the phone back. Eyes still on lock.

"You really taking me in, huh? It's like you looking at my soul with those eyes of yours, girl," Jaka smiled. Again with no words. Tashi reluctantly broke the gaze to glance down at her phone. "Jaka, huh? Great name. It's..."

"It's homemade. Thanks. My pops is Chaka and, you guessed it, my mom was Jackie."

Tashi smiled back, "Of course. Very nice to meet you. Mine is short for Natasha. Let's link sometime soon."

"I gave you the flyer, but that was kind of for me," Tashi continued, laughing lightly. "You gave me your number...which is for both of us. Let me give you something that's for you."

And with that she took a set of plastic love beads from around her neck and placed them around Jaka's. Jaka immediately fingered the beads and could not help but wonder about the excitement that awaited her.

10 Akhaji Zakiya

1

Jaka - "Tall Chocolatte, Shaken ...and Stirred"

"Take your positions to move across the floor, please."

Music and movement filled Studio B as Jaka peeked in to do a headcount. Only seven students were in this week's class, and there were only eight in last week's. Rhythmnation had been her passion project and life's work ever since she took it over as part of the settlement with Michael in their split seven years ago. Jaka ran the dance studio/rehearsal space which specialized in West African, Latin and urban dance traditions. She also served as artistic director of the studio's popular dance ensemble. Often referred to as a 'tall, chocolate shake', Jaka was a 5'9 beauty with electric eyes that spoke volumes. When she was responding to the call of the drum, she lost herself and took audiences, willing captives, on her mesmerizing ride.

Having a rootsy dad, who selected for Bloodfyah Sound since before Jaka could read, developed her appreciation for conscious reggae and message-laced soca. In her teens, her musical tastes trended toward house music, afrobeat and the dancehall variety of reggae. She still loved the driving bass and urgent rhythms of dancehall. Every now and then she dragged Nina, her long-time best friend and the dance studio's manager, to a show - Movado, Chronixx or whoever was in town. Staying connected to derivatives of the culture she grew up with allowed her to hold her own with the young dancers in the company, even though next month she would officially be in her late thirties. Last year when a young company member approached her and Nina about starting a dancehall/West African fusion class, they were all for it.

The new class started with standing room only a few weeks ago and now was down to just seven students. Jaka could not help but feel disappointed and a bit worried. As she closed the door to the studio, she lamented silently that something needed to be done about getting more dancers, and wanna-be dancers, in all classes. While some funds came through performance fees, grants and donations, the majority of Rhythmnation's income was from evening and weekend classes for children, teens and adults. In the past few months, the studio had faced financial challenges that were threatening Jaka's three-year plan to buy the building when the lease expired. In the short-term, it was getting more difficult to pay great instructors, especially those specializing in popular forms.

Jaka smiled at Tim in the wall of mirrors across from the door. He was a well-liked instructor and they were lucky to have him. She needed to project positivity in the face of uncertainty.

"Have a good class you all," Jaka closed the door and headed down the hall, musing on ideas to bring more funds into the studio. They could install poles and go the strippercise route. Or charge a fee to attend rehearsals as there seemed to be no shortage of creeps wanting to 'watch', or rather, drool over company members. She thought of this idea often, despite the lecherous implications. Jaka knew a lot of her dad's friends would pay to drool – she had dealt with a lot of that inappropriateness growing up.

"Bwoy, Chaka," they would say to her dad, "Dat is one thick and healthy something you got dere, man. She sweet! She mussi favour she mama."

After years of being ogled, and even propositioned, by some of her dad's friends, Jaka was ready to be married at sixteen just so that they would stop. She married at nineteen instead. She and Michael went on to dance magic together at home and on stage for over ten years.

Jaka strode to the small kitchen just past the reception area to fill her water bottle before finding an empty studio to work on the choreography for Rhythmnation's upcoming annual season. The phone rang as she passed Nina at the front desk. A loyal friend and valuable manager, Nina was very proud of her Sri Lankan roots and her early training in classical Indian dance traditions. She became a lover of all things Latina as she got older. Her admiration of the culture, salsa, reggaeton and *paella* in particular, was evident to all. Combined with her caramel complexion, loosely-curled mass of dark hair and curvy, solid figure often led people to mistakenly identify her as Latina.

"Hello. Rhythmnation Dance Studio," Nina answered in her professional voice reserved for the office.

"Jaka?" Nina caught her friend's attention and asked with her eyebrows if she wanted to take the call. Jaka shook her head and continued down the hall. She was ready to shift her emotional energy from nagging worry to creative inspiration. 'A good sweat wouldn't hurt either,' she thought as she exhaled and closed the studio door behind her.

"Yes, Jaka is in the studio, but she's not available right now. Might I take a message? Right, okay….A duet, huh? Especially for the occasion, with lots of, um…right. Okay. Lots of detail…um, don't know how well topless will go over? Yes, well we can always sort out wardrobe at a later time. Right…I'll be sure to relay the message. Thanks, bye."

Nina hung up and bee-lined to Studio A where Jaka had her left leg on the barre and was facing the mirrors while touching her forehead to her knee.

"Lady, you will not believe who just called," Nina had a knack for blowing the mundane out of proportion, so Jaka did not get excited.

"Okay, tell me, nuh?" Jaka replied while swinging her left ankle past her ear, holding her leg in vertical position and pulling it to the ceiling. Nina, who had always admired Jaka's grace, flexibility and sheer sexiness could not help but pass her eyes over the meeting of her thighs.

"The fiancées want you, lady," Nina exclaimed.

"What?"

"The Denises want you to perform...at their wedding...in the Barbados!"

"It's 'Barbados', Nina. Not 'the Barbados'."

"I know, I know...I added it for emphasis," she joked. "Hey, isn't your dad from there?

"No, he's from Tobago, remember? It's my mom's people. They are in Barbados."

"Right, right. All those small islands are alike. Easy to get confused." Nina teased her friend.

Jaka replied, "You are from an island too, girl. Granted yours, your parents' to be exact, is a much bigger island. Like more than 100 times bigger." Nina giggled in response.

"Hmmm…" Jaka wondered out loud as she released the leg, turned to her side and proceeded to rotate it back and forth in its socket. "Okay. The fiancées want to fly us there to perform one piece?"

"Yes, dark Denise said they want to commission a special, contemporary-styled duet that reflects their 'love journey'. Yuck!"

Nina touched her fingers to her lips and heaved a little as if she was going to throw up. "Of course they'll want to talk to you, show you pics, review music options. Apparently they are thinking of a Ledisi song opened by Latin and African drumming. And lady, are you ready for this? You are so not ready. Okay, like you and your naming of this place they are inspired by Ms. Jackson-if-you-nasty," Nina giggled uncontrollably. "They've got some, ah, wardrobe suggestions…that involve you…and the other dancer…that's right, baring those titties, lady. They said they figured it was more authentic this way!" Nina hardly finished the sentence before collapsing into fits of laughter.

"Yeah, right," Jaka said. "I don't know about this…sounds a little creepy to me," Nina smiled and shook her head in mock disbelief.

"This coming from you who wants to pimp out company members to your Dad's friends?

Please. Did I mention they have a budget and are willing to pay our regular rate?"

"Really? Do they know how much that is?" Now Jaka was starting to get interested.

"Lady, you know how dark Denise is loaded. It may not be hers but that chick sure knows how to tap into her family's funds. Do you know they are picking up the tab for the wedding?"

"Wow. Interesting. I can't believe her Caribbean family is into this gay wedding business."

"Seems so, lady. The ceremony will be held at the family estate on the west coast, she said. Apparently a lot of light Denise's people are flying in too."

"Nina, why do you insist on calling them dark and light Denise? It's so..."

"So what am I to call them...by their last names? That doesn't make any sense because they'll both be Clarke-Addae soon anyway. Besides everybody describes them like that."

"Wait a minute. You mean, they both are going to have the exact same name now? That's crazy! Why would they hyphenate their last names and then both use the same name? Talk about crazy lezzie bonding. That's just too much. So except for their complexions.... Nina, please tell me these two soon-to-be-married, grown-ass women are not going to have the exact same name?!"

"But it's easier for the children."

"Oh my, gosh. I'm done!" Jaka exploded in incredulity while dropping into the splits and beginning the floor work part of her warm-up.

"We are queer," she extra annunciated. "Can't we just love loving pussy, and of course women or whatever, and just be done with it? This marriage and two point seven kids crap traditional trend that's going around can really ruin the cool, free-loving queer vibe that folks have given their lives for."

"Now, that's intense. Stop hating, Jaka. And you better not let your girl hear you talking like that," Nina said with a sly smile.

"I know, right? I'm already dreading how all this wedding talk is going to get Tashi all riled up and hinting again. Don't know if my nerves can take it right now...not with all the money pressure we've been feeling around here lately."

"Lady, you are still as phobic as hell...commitment-phobic that is! You better put a ring on it before somebody else does. What's it been, like three years in a lesbian relationship? Damn, that's a long-ass time in the regular world. You better figure that out! Anyway, don't you worry about the money stuff, Jaka. Enrollment will pick back up with the warm weather and we'll get past this. You know, the duet could be just the hot cash injection we need," Nina thrusted her hips forward and rolled them in a grinding motion to simulate her point.

"Whatever, Nina. Go on with your rudeness. Well, you may be right, but don't go chatting all this to Tashi, okay. I need a moment to think about it."

Truth be known, Jaka was hesitant to truly expose all of her heart, all of her. That was what dance was for. There flowing in between the rhythms and melodies of movement, in between time and space, she could easily share her heart's beats in ensemble or solo. Enveloping everyone in the dance and around it. Meditative movement opened her heart, and often her soul. Folks could feel it as they experienced her on stage.

The dance studio and creative collaboration with other artists was Jaka's definitive comfort zone. Sometimes she struggled to share her feelings as easily in her personal relations. With Nina it was different because it often felt like they shared the same brain. They could be so similar in their outlooks on life. In addition to their use of dance to release emotion and communicate without words. Sometimes, truth be known, they used the art to escape too. In the almost three years they had been together, Jaka often felt that Tashi wanted more than she could give. Whether it was to be closer to Tashi's large family – Haitian on one side, Venezuelan on the other - or be more politically engaged around human rights issues. Jaka remained focused on the dance. As if she could feel Jaka thinking about her, just then Tashi appeared at the door.

"Hey baby, hey Nina," she greeted. "Oh sweetheart, your stuff looks so good in that position!" Tashi, still excited by the sight of her lover, hurried over to Jaka, who was on her back. She got on all fours to kiss her lips. Tashi was a curious blend of regality and goofiness. Her broad shoulders and narrow hips worked well on her medium-sized frame. It was very hard to miss her in a room. Largely due to her signature wild afro that framed her cute face.

"So, what is it you need to think about?" Tashi asked innocently, looking first at Jaka, then at Nina as she prepared to head back to reception. Jaka shot her friend a 'shut your mouth' look as Nina moved to the door.

"Nothing, babes. Come give a proper squeeze." Tashi removed her coat and set it next to her purse on a nearby chair, before making her way back to Jaka.

She loved to watch her sweetheart do her thing on the dance floor. Any dance floor. After the kiss and hug hello, she returned to the back of the room and sat cross-legged facing the mirrors. Tashi wanted to see Jaka's reflection as she warmed up in preparation for several run-throughs of the three solos she would be performing at the upcoming show.

As she pressed the remote to fill the studio with the sounds of Femi Kuti and Janelle Monae, Jaka caught her lover's eye. She touched her tongue to her top lip and flashed her eyes across the room. Tashi felt warm. Instantly. She resisted a sharp urge to crawl over to Jaka and lay her out on the middle of the floor. Instead she winked and slowly pushed out her bottom lip. Her mind floated to the love they had shared last Sunday afternoon when she vowed to rub her lips over every part of Jaka's exquisite body. Reflecting back to the wonder of their passionate coming together, she smiled remembering that she had missed a few parts after becoming pre-occupied with other parts. This memory made her smile on the inside, too.

She watched Jaka spin twice, stop suddenly, take five slow steps backward then throw both arms up, fists clenched, back straight. Then she slowly sunk to the floor. Dramatically relaxing each vertebrae as if it were not connected to one another. She melted into a tightly, curled ball. Her face reflected her body's contracted movement. It morphed from buoyant to trouble-filled to hopeful. Tashi marveled at the range of emotions in her gestures, her expressions. It was such a joy to watch her partner's facial movements complement the energy of the story her body was telling. It was easy to see that Jaka loved dance. So much so that she lived in it most of the time. Spoke in it even. Tashi often wished that Jaka was as expressive in their relationship as she was when dancing. It could sometimes take several attempts and boundless patience on Tashi's part to get at the heart of their disagreements.

Dance was definitely Jaka's world. Through creating pieces of art that moved her audiences, she shared her world and wanted others to enjoy. Tashi wanted to enjoy her woman fully. Right now. She had heard when Nina locked the front door on her way out with Tim after making sure all the dancehall/West African fusion students had left. They were alone. Jaka was shiny with sweat and Tashi wanted to lick those parts she did not get to last time.

She walked over to her boo when Jaka had stopped moving for a moment.

"I want you," was all she whispered as they touched lips. Before Jaka could intensify the light kiss, Tashi was on her knees brushing her lips across Jaka's stomach and nibbling on the top of her tights.

"I'm yours right now, babes. Could use a break anyway," Jaka replied as she unconsciously tensed her body in anticipation of the certain pleasure that was to come. Tashi's mouth hovered over the top of Jaka's thong. Her hands stroked hard thighs, eyes deep into her lover's. Tashi wanted to drag off the tights, thong while grabbing Jaka's ass and feeding off her juice like a thick slice of watermelon. She resisted.

"That's right," Tashi breathed through a well-placed kiss. "You most definitely are.

That's why you are going to stand there so I can lick those parts I missed on Sunday," Tashi could feel her inner freak rising. While Jaka was not much for words, she loved to be spoken to during sex. "And then, and then I'm gonna love you sweetly with my mouth until you beg me to get up inside you and make you feel it a different way. And then you know what's gonna happen?" Tashi breathed the question into Jaka's left hip, while running her hands deliberately up and down the back of firm thighs. Jaka was distracted from rehearsing, but happy for the surprise love break. Tashi had her stuff wet, beyond the effects of dancing. Slippery wet. The kind you want to share. Jaka got near-instantly aroused when Tashi talked nasty to her even after all these years. Being in the studio with her tights hanging off her ass and her sexy lover's mouth hovering around her sweet spot was perfect right now. It had been too long of a worrisome day. Jaka did not have a witty reply.

"This feels so good, baby. The anticipation…tell me what's gonna happen. What you gonna do to me?" she mumbled. On her knees and loving it, Tashi looked up into Jaka eyes and desire flowed through her gaze. Tashi wanted her lover to feel how much she was wanted. She longed to dive right in and have her way with the moist folds of flesh in front of her face. She wanted to press her mouth on top, then slide down, stroking with her tongue. She intended to make Jaka enjoy every bit of how excited she got when watching her dance or even just move through a room. Tashi was going to show her exactly how she felt. Slowly. Then do it again.

"I love this, baby," She mouthed into Jaka's precious parts. Jaka moaned hard and grabbed Tashi's shoulder with one hand. She started to push her head closer, when Tashi resisted. She pushed back against the hand and slid her mouth further down Jaka's thigh, kissing and licking as she went.

"Delicious," she whispered into soft, smooth skin. "I'm gonna so savour every moment of this, baby. It's not often we get down in the studio." Jaka's hand loosened its grip and brushed over Tashi's cheek. She sighed as her body relaxed into the love she was receiving. She felt her insides pour down, juicily revealing her eagerness. She wanted to grind her stuff all over her lover's lips. Instead she exhaled slowly and tried to not push Tashi's face into her ready moistness. On the intake, she tingled and felt warmth rise from her core. She was going to take it just as Tashi loved to give it – slow and deep, then fast and sweaty, then everything in between. Jaka knew that if she relaxed into Tashi's steady, deliberate waves, her body would be rewarded repeatedly. She sighed and focused on Tashi's magical mouth. It was trailing down her thigh again. This time first down to her right knee, then her left. Lightly kissing and licking back up her legs, Tashi firmly squeezed Jaka's ass with intent. Her mouth breezed over hips and lightly landed where Jaka's lower hairline began. Kisses and licks intensified into tiny bites and sucks. It was on.

"Let me taste," Tashi murmured gesturing with her chin and pulling back to look up for a reaction.

"Get it, Tashi!" Jaka urged, pulling her tights down and slipping out one foot. Returning upright, she could not stop her hips from bucking forward and revealing her arousal. First, she brushed her attentive clit against Tashi's lips. She sucked passionately and pressed her hands against Jaka's roundness. Then Jaka held the back of Tashi's head, angling her hips and spreading her legs so that the protruding tongue would land at her opening. She wanted Tashi to get her entire mouth wet. Sweet sensations shot through her body as Tashi rolled her tongue and slid it deeper inside.

Jaka growled as the tongue treat got faster. Tashi's top lip was pressed down deliciously on her hood. 'So good!' they thought simultaneously. Jaka could feel herself expanding even more under the sweet pressure. She wanted to bust. She knew that if she relaxed, even though her legs, ass and ab muscles were clenched, and kept breathing and did not move her hips too much, she could hold her orgasms and let them build into bigger expressions. The more her clit popped, the harder and longer she would come. Tashi was skilled at working her body, specifically all parts of her pussy. She often joked that Tashi was the choreographer in the bedroom. Or the dance studio, as it were. Remembering where she was, Jaka opened her eyes and looked briefly around the room before looking down. Tashi's face was pumping. Wet lips wrapped tightly around Jaka's now-enormous bud.

"Oh my, Tashi. You a fierce, fucking beast! Look how you get me so excited…oh, and about to come. You gonna keep sucking me like that, honey? Oh my! You gonna keep doing that? Get that!"

Tashi smiled and deliberately dragged her tongue over Jaka's opening to taste her again. Jaka gripped the sides of Tashi head and felt coils of hair squeeze through her fingers. She was moving now, rocking to Tashi's rhythms, matching her mouth stokes with hip thrusts.

They became one when Jaka busted and screamed. Tashi kept pumping with her lips. She loved feeling her lover's essence in her mouth as she came. It danced a little every time. Shook from side to side at first, then shimmied in circles as her breathing slowed to resting state. Tashi was not quite ready to end the spontaneous session in the studio. She knew her lover's body. Jaka still had muscles clenched and was muttering repeatedly, "Fuck, that was good," as she remained standing and tried to compose herself.

Both hands held Tashi's shoulders now. Her mouth was still lightly touching Jaka's pulsating clit. One hand clenched a butt cheek. The fingers on her other massaged Jaka's outer lips and were moving inside. Before Jaka could mumble one more exclamation of pleasure, she groaned deep and low as Tashi's fullness inside caught her off guard. She had slipped two fingers into Jaka's centre while still gently brushing her mouth on her clit. Tashi felt herself drench. She was never quite sure which she liked more - being on or in. Moments like these were everything because she did not have to decide. She loved having her mouth and hands full of Jaka. She felt very connected to her in these moments.

Jaka loved it too. Especially when she was recovering from one enchanting orgasm and could feel the next one mounting. She loved feeling Tashi rub up her wet walls...fingers sliding in and around with purpose. She could sense Tashi's desire to feel all of her in every stroke. Every thrust ended (and began) with pointed pressure up against her sweet spot. Just a hint at first. Then Tashi pushed in, pressed up and, as a reward, Jaka's bud popped, tingled and gratified her expectant lips. Her opening fluttered and her walls contracted gripping her lover close. Tashi clenched in expectation of sharing in Jaka's next orgasm. Whether music was on or not, she adored making her woman's pussy dance...from the outside and the inside.

2

Nina - "And the Beat Goes On"

As she made her way down the stairs from the dance studio, Nina floated onto the sidewalk ready for the next part of her day.

"Those two are something else!" She chuckled under her breath. "One minute they are arguing about if they should move in together, the next they are all googly eyes like they haven't seen each other in years. Ah, the joys of relationships." She grinned, grateful that her life - for the moment – did not suffer the vertigo of those ups and downs. "Better get a room," she muttered. Then remembered they had one. Knowing her friend, they were probably enjoying each other right now.

Akhaji Zakiya

Nina shook her head, inhaled the evening air and reflected on how far Jaka had come. How she had blossomed into an assured woman, how now sex seeped from her with inviting ease. They had known each other since the first year of the professional program at the Headley School for Dance. Both majored in Modern with a focus on Urban dance. They shared classes, shows and change rooms. Since those sweaty, insecure, uber-competitive days, Nina and Jaka had grown to love each other like the sister never they had. By the time Nina was pregnant, Jaka was the only real, non-family choice for godmother of Carlos, her nine-year-old son. But when they first met sparks flew, and not in a good way.

Dance had always been a big part of Nina's life. While she did not have a problem speaking her mind when she had to, dancing helped channel a lot of her feelings in a positive way. As a single parent who grew up in a noisy, argument-filled household, Nina was committed to not raising her voice in anger toward Carlos. Sometimes she just needed to shake off the frustration and found dance, especially salsa, was great for that. On stage, her presence was enthralling. It more than made up for any technical imprecision. The audience felt her essence. And she captured their eyes. At the club, she was the life of the party. Any party. Nina was known for dominating the dance floor by starting trends and re-enacting moves from popular music videos. By the end of the song, she would have transformed it into something all her own, a creation that everyone had no choice but to imitate.

Recognizing her natural movement ability and sense of rhythm from an early age, Nina's parents, both lovers of the arts, exposed her to classical Indian dance training and piano lessons. As she approached her teens and became more certain she wanted to explore dance as a career, her parents allowed her to take additional classes in tap and modern. She was a tap dancing natural.

She loved being able to make her own music with her body. Often she pretended to drum *tabla* with her feet when going in with her tap shoes on. Nina used tap so much as a form of expression that more than one lover had encouraged her to use her words versus loud, intricate tap sequences when communicating during an argument. She and Jaka often laughed about this. Like Nina, Jaka understood that sometimes, when you do not want to shout things that can never be unsaid, its best to dance. Or something. Nina's last serious lover did not get this and refused to call for days after Nina composed a spontaneous, eleven-minute jazz tap number one afternoon while the couple was discussing why they did not spend more time together.

*　*　*

When Nina first met Jaka, all she saw was another stuck-up dancer/"artiste" who was full of herself. Jaka arrived at the prestigious Headley School from an elite arts high school in the west end. She walked with her head held high, did not seem to have many friends and hardly made eye contact. It was rare to hear her speak. But she was always early and at the front of every class they shared. Because of her outstanding form and technique, Jaka was often the instructor's go-to student to demonstrate moves.

At that time, Nina honestly found her hard to like and even harder to avoid. Jaka was everywhere. On campus committees, starring in the spring and fall performance showcases, heading up dance student council and often, surprisingly, at all the hot parties. Nina always figured that since Jaka was such an arts nerd snob, her social coolness (and the hot party invites) were because of her very delicious fiancée, Michael.

While a student dancer, Nina was not-so-affectionately referred to, by acquaintances and friends, as a 'raving lesbian bent on conversion.' Those days Nina was all about the female form. As dancers it was not unusual to be naked around women. Nina always had a banging, flexible body and knew what to do with it. Back then she did not believe in wasting it on guys. She was infamous for saying that dudes were too easy, a dime a dozen.

Back then a real challenge for her was getting an unsuspecting woman to share herself. Nina found it sweeter when the woman did not know she wanted to and had never shared her treats with another woman before. Back then she put a spin on the 'nothing-better-than-new-pussy' phrase.

Needless to say, this orientation and behavior pissed off and embarrassed Nina's parents, a Singhalese dentist and his Tamil admin assistant wife. Her outspoken sexuality and reputation for flirting inappropriately did not endear her to her classmates either. Especially not Jaka and most of the other star dancers. They regarded Nina as way too over-the-top. Despite their differences, the two eventually connected over a piece of music and became friendly after a crazy night at a house music party.

Jaka loved the track that Nina had used for a solo in their second-year Contemporary Fusion class. For the assignment, students were encouraged to blend dance and music styles unconventionally. Nina threw down tight tap riffs and fluid, salsa-inspired moves over, under and in-between a well-produced *bhangra*-reggaeton house mix with a soul-penetrating bass line. Students went wild when she finished what felt like an emotionally-telling offering of her raw, polished talent.

In the change room after class, Jaka walked up behind Nina as she was pulling on a sweater and asked about the musical artist on the track. Nina was a little startled at first. Partly because she did not hear Jaka as she approached, but also because Jaka was actually talking to her. Her reply was cool, as usual.

"Hey, yeah it's a really great mix, huh? My cousin blended it special for me after I told him the sounds and tempos I wanted. He's a DJ. I'll have to get back to you on the names of the artists," she explained.

Jaka nodded in response.

"He spins Indo, Latino, Afro-infused house at various spots around town, but usually on Thursdays at The Drop. You should check it out," Nina continued slightly flirtatiously. She was still surprised they were speaking. Suggestive comments and eye-brow indications had become her regular way of engaging women. Especially beautiful ones like Ms. Perfect "I am an Artiste above all" Jaka. 'Whatever,' Nina thought. 'She came over to talk to me.'

"Good to know, I'll tell Michael about it. I love house music," Jaka said. As she turned to walk back to her locker, she added, "You killed it today as you know. Have a good next class."

"Thanks!" Nina could not keep the disbelief at the compliment out of her tone. Maybe she was a not complete diva princess, she considered for the first time.

The following Thursday, despite the downpour, Nina made it to the infamous Thursday night club. The plan was to meet a group of friends there for birthday drinks and kicking up their feet. Her queer girl crew had recently stopped limiting themselves to only lesbian events. They were, according to Jessie, leader of the crew, about sharing their love across the fluid lines of sexual diversity. The group's own spin on "We're here, we are queer" was to get folks used to it by taking up space where they were not always expected. Like at a house music night in the club district.

'Strange,' Nina thought as she waited for the light to change. 'Because house music was created by working-class, Black gay men. But these days techno, trance, trip-hop, tribal and other derivatives seem to have taken over the genre.' That night featured four different DJs and promised to take the crowd back to original vibes.

Nina's crew was usually seven or eight deep and easy to spot because of their funky hairstyles and unique style of dress. When she arrived at the gate that evening, there was a mass of people standing near the entrance, behind the customary red-velvet rope. They formed in a disorderly, near-line configuration, huddled trying to not get wet. Three black-clad bouncers, tall as oaks, talked to one another under the canopy just outside the door. Nina scanned the crowd, then concluded that her friends were already inside. To confirm her hunch, she quickly pulled out her phone. There was a text from Jessie.

Nina replied, *'coming. outside wet in stupid line'* before returning it to her pocket. After a few moments, she noticed that people were being selected from the assembled crowd based on their appearance and apparent familiarity with the door guys instead of the actual time they had been waiting.

'Oh, no way I'm having this tonight,' she thought to herself. 'I did not come out my house to get wet and pay to get in!' She grabbed her phone again to text her cousin so he could finesse the bouncers. She finished her five-word text *'come get me at door!'* and tried not to let her frustration show.

In her tight mini-skirt, heeled sandals and sequined crop top, she had not dressed to be in the rain and, of course, her purse was too small to hold an umbrella. Her cousin had promised to put her name at the door, but with this crowd it was best he just come to the gate. Quickly. As Nina was about to hit send when her phone died.

'Damn!' she thought. 'Any other day that low battery light flashes for hours.' Damp now and not sure what best to do, Nina wondered which bouncer was most likely to recognize her as DJ Lanka's cousin. She sighed and remembered she was there to celebrate a buddy and to have a good time with her girls. A little water and waiting were not going to mess up her night. She picked the bouncer to approach and fixed a smile on her face. As she moved toward him, she saw Jaka, Michael and another dancer from school. Nina stopped walking because she was somewhat stunned to see them. She watched the three ease through the crowd and right up to the security guys. Michael was shaking hands and pump-hugging his buddies at the door when Nina arrived beside them.

"Hey, lady!" she exclaimed, still a bit shocked, but happy to see them. Even more so because it seemed they had an in to the club. 'Imagine that! And I'm the one who told Jaka about it last week,' she marveled silently at the irony. When Jaka saw Nina, she smiled warmly and touched her forearm in greeting. Then she introduced Nina to Michael and her good friend, Nicole.

"Sweet you guys could make it. My people are in already. Let's make this party fly!" They did. Until the last song played, and the lights came on. By the end of the night, right there on that dance floor, Jaka and Nina had become friends.

* * *

It was a sunny, spring evening. Nina was glad to get out of the Rhythmnation studio for the day and feel the warm breeze on her face. She was early for her yoga class, so decided to walk the seven blocks instead of riding the train. Hot yoga was the third biggest love of her life. The first, of course, was Carlos, then dance, her life's dedication. After those two, sex was next on the list…or maybe hot yoga. Depending on what was going on in her life. In some ways, the practice of hot yoga was sensual for her, in a solitary, spiritual way. When she was in her yogi zone, Nina stared into her own eyes reflected in the mirrors and barely noticed anyone else in the room. For her, it was one of those experiences where she was by herself yet in communion with others. The group moved and breathed together for ninety minutes in a moist, heated room that reminded her of the rainforest. She loved the soothing caress every bit of her body, mind and soul felt after a good class. Like dance, it also helped release emotion.

As far as Nina was concerned, hot yoga came into her life at the perfect time over ten years ago when a friend from high school introduced it to her. She credited the practice - the breathing, being present and silent in your body, being alone but not by herself, the cleansing of the sweat - for saving her life. At that time, things in her world had become very bleak. She was separating from her ex, her first real love, and hot yoga was just what she needed to take her mind off the drama of it all. These days she appreciated that the deep, extended stretches and relaxation balanced the wear and tear of years of dancing on her 36-year old self. Along with what she called her 'spiritual exercise,' Nina believed firmly in taking very good care of herself. She found a way to finance regular deep-tissue massage and acupuncture treatments as well as prepare healthy meals for her and Carlos. After all, her body was her business.

Tonight she was instructing class. Guiding really, she liked to think of it. Contributing to the environment by facilitating people through the twenty-six standard postures. She had covered the seven blocks in no time. When she arrived at the reception area of the yoga studio, she tucked her purse and sports bag under the L-shaped desk where her co-worker sat.

"Hey, Kate. How are you? Sure is packed in here today."

"Hi, Nina. I know, right? Class doesn't start for fifteen minutes, and all the spots are almost gone!"

"Wow, some folks are going to be pissed if they don't get here soon," Nina said while peeking through the small window in the door to the yoga studio. "Thought the nice weather we are having might keep people away."

"Yeah, right. People are getting themselves summer ready, my friend," Kate replied. It was probably true. Next to dance training or crazy-expensive Pilates there were few forms of activity that could whip a body into shape quite like hot yoga. Nina loved it when football guys came to class as part of their preparation for the season. 'Maybe it was all the sweating and emotional release,' Nina wondered to herself. It was not for everybody, but it was effective.

"You might be right," Nina laughed. Kate was always so kind and knowledgeable. Nina enjoyed working with her.

"I already got my spot," Kate asserted as she looked right at Nina and slid her a grin.

"Great, because looks like 'snooze you lose' in there right now," Nina joked.

"I got one right up front."

Nina did not get to respond because she felt her phone buzz in the pocket of her fitted jacket. She mouthed to Kate that she had to take the call and moved to the windows at the far left of the reception area for privacy. The buzz turned out to be a text from her brother's phone instead of the call she expected it to be.

'hey, Ma practice wz awesome. playin left forward on Sat! goin back with twins and uncle D now for food.'

Nina laughed at the attached picture. Each of the three boys was trying to take the soccer ball away from her brother. One of the twins was on his back, arms outstretched. The other was draped over his left leg in a body grip intended to slow his father down. Carlos, not much for the roughhousing, faced his uncle with a foot darting out in an attempt to at least touch the ball, if not steal it away. David was 6'2, lean, muscled and cat-quick. Even years after his soccer scholarships had paid for school, he still managed to play a couple of nights a week. He also took the boys to their under-12 league practice on Tuesdays and Thursdays. Nina took them to most of their Saturday morning games. Jay was an only child, so it was good for him to be with his older cousins. She noticed him developing a nurturing, sharing side that was so important for any kid, especially a boy.

David was a fantastic father and, knowing that his nephew's dad was not around, he went out of his way to make sure he extended his love to Carlos. It mattered to him that the pre-teen felt included in family activities. The arrangement was a blessing because it allowed her to teach yoga on both of those nights. Plus Carlos got dropped home feeling exhausted with just enough energy to review his homework before falling out. As a small token of her appreciation, Nina sent cooked food, parceled out in individually-labelled plastic containers, for David and the boys every week.

She was pleased to see all the fun being had in the picture. The weather had finally warmed, and the children were taking every opportunity to be outside. Of course, they were video game fiends, like many their age. But David and Nina always encouraged walks, sports, picnics, beach days, camping and lots of outdoor activities to stimulate them and ease the challenges of single-parenthood.

As she returned to the desk, it occurred to Nina that while the texted picture was cute, it was strange. Carlos would usually call her from the car after soccer practice, not text. 'Hmmm,' she wondered. 'And who took the photo?' Her inner detective was feeling like something might not be adding up. She decided to call back the phone, hoping that Carlos might answer since David was driving. After three rings, he did. She heard loud voices over top-forty music in the background.

"Hi pumpkin head, how are you? Thanks for the pic."

"I'm good, ma. Just tired and hungry from running. We getting burgers soon."

"Okay, I'm glad you're getting to play your fave position on Saturday. You're going to be awesome."

"Thanks, ma. I will!"

"So burgers, huh? That's a treat. But I left food for all four of you in the freezer when we were over on the weekend. Remember?"

"Yeah, but there are five of us. And she's getting the burgers."

Nina had known something was up! In the picture, David was bending over, but looking into the camera. With a gleam in his eye. Nina knew her brother, and she had not seen that look for a very long time.

"Oh, I see, pumpkin. Someone else is there with you?"

"Yeah, ma she's..." and then the call dropped before he could finish his sentence. Frustrated by the timing of poor service, she started to call back when her phone buzzed in her hand.

'*See you later, sexy pants?*'

Nina sighed and put the phone away without replying to the text or calling back. She grabbed her sports bag and headed to the instructor change room. It was time to focus on class. Besides, as much as she loved a good late-night hook up, this particular situation was feeling dragged out and tired. Slipping into her yoga costume of short shorts and, essentially, a bikini top, Nina put on her slippers and padded down the hall. She cracked open the door to the hot room and stepped into the moisture being sure to close it behind her. Most students were lying face up; toes pointed to the back wall, on towels positioned over yoga mats. Some were already standing, some stretching, others fidgeting while they faced the mirrored wall at the front of the room.

Nina stayed in her meditative, self-focused practice when she took class. But as an instructor, she moved around the almost-steamy room and sometimes gave corrections (as they say in the dance world) or suggestions (more appropriate for yoga) depending on how many people were in class. When Nina was instructing, the walk-arounds only happened during the first part of class. By the time they got to 'triangle forehead to knee', the middle posture of the series, most participants were dripping and all towels were soaked to some degree. At the end of some crowded classes, almost all of the exposed studio floor would be wet making it difficult to walk safely.

For most of Nina's friends, especially Jaka for some reason, the mere thought of a sealed, hot room of forty-plus people deep breathing ("Where does all that exhale go?") and perspiring into puddles not absorbed by over-saturated towels ("A shallow pool of other people's sweat?!") while in their underwear was not how they wanted to spend any hour and a half of their life. Despite extolling its virtues over the years, she could not get them to try it.

Maybe it was because she was born under the water element in Chinese astrology and was a Scorpio in the western tradition. Or because she was used to rubbing bodies with sweaty dancers for many years. For whatever reason, Nina did not mind the moisture. She found it cleansing, as long as she did not have to do the mopping up afterward. Gladly, Kate would handle that tonight. After class and this long day, Nina looked forward to heading home for hugs with Carlos as he told her the details of his time away from her. Then they would review his homework before he had his bath and went to bed. She expected him to be exhausted after running around and playing with his cousins. But she would be sure to ask him about who was in the car and buying them burgers.

Once he was tucked in, she could relax with a glass of red and get into her steamy, erotic novel. She had left off at a good place the night before. As she planned the next few hours in her mind during the final breathing exercises and *Savasana* that allowed taxed bodies to return to resting state, Nina remembered the text she had glanced just before class.

"What great energy and effort in here today. Feel the effects flowing through you," Nina said softly to the winded, dripping group laying in front of her. "Enjoy the rest of your day. *Namaste*."

She had opened the studio door earlier to let air in. As Nina stepped back into the relatively cool reception area and considered what her response to the text invitation should be. 'Do I really want company tonight?' she mused. Sometimes she arranged for certain lovers to swing by well after Carlos was asleep. It was a privilege afforded very few on the condition that they did not spend the night. That kind of intimacy Nina strictly reserved. At this moment in her life, there was no one in that category. Although many had tried, including the sender of the text she still did not know how to respond to.

She ducked into the shower for a quick rinse. As she rubbed her body with lavender soap lathered by her loofah and enjoyed the gentle beating of warm water cleansing off her day, Nina realized that while she was always up for hot sex with no (real) strings, she wanted to pass for tonight. She loved loving herself and, along with her juicy Fiona Zedde novel, she would be good. Plus her glass of wine, of course.

'*Weekend rain check?*' Nina texted back after drying her hair and dressing.

'*Awww ;(*' flashed on the screen before she could return the phone to its designated spot in her purse.

'*Sho?*' appeared as Nina considered how to be firm yet gentle, still leaving the door open for a possible weekend visit.

'*Sho? Sho?*' she read before the keypad could pop up for her to type a response. It was at times like this that Nina could feel her lover's youth. After all, she understood, if only by the comments and reactions of others, that she was considered sexy. But this evening of sharing, as she and Jaka liked to call it, would have to wait.

'*Sho, sho, hun. Def hit me up on Sat tho*'

'*K,*' was the one-word reply.

'I'll deal with that on the weekend,' Nina reasoned with herself. She had her boots on now and was looking forward to getting home at least a few minutes before her brother dropped off Carlos. She bounced down the steps of the building and headed toward the train station. Turning to walk, she noticed someone waving and smiling at her from across the street. The dark-skinned man had his hair cut low and wore stylish, thick-rimmed glasses. His light grey suit was close fitting. Cherry brown shoes reflected the glow of the setting sun and went well with the suit. Nina noticed fashion everywhere she went. He looked well-put together, but she still did not recognize who he was. It was not a coincidence he was there. This was revealed to her later.

"How you doing, Nina. It's me Patrice," he said as he crossed the street toward her.

"Oh Patrice," she replied. "I barely recognized you in your work drag."

"True, you always see me in sweats and sweaty. This is how I do when I'm on the grind," he laughed and tapped both hands to his chest. "Had to put in extra hours today…big delivery deadlines are coming up. Would have liked to have been your class tonight," he said while shifting the overcoat he was carrying from his right forearm to his left so he could shake her hand in greeting. He figured a hug would have been too familiar. After all, she was only his yoga instructor and Patrice was just getting to know her, so he did not want to push it. Not just yet anyway. He liked the way she grinned at him. The other four times they had been in each other's company, he had been in his yoga costume – fitted shorts like the ones he had on under his suit, but made out of a synthetic blend to resist moisture.

'What a blessed, serendipitous moment this is,' he thought. He was hoping that he would get to see this lovely lady. Over the past few months, Patrice had developed a noticeable crush on Nina. She had experienced this before with students both in yoga and dance. She sensed exactly when it happened with Patrice.

To enhance understanding, instructors were encouraged to occasionally take three or four minutes to demonstrate, or have a student demonstrate, one of the twenty-six postures of the series. About three weeks ago, Nina was showing in detail the 'standing separate leg stretching' posture. It begins with placing the legs about three feet apart and fully extending arms from the shoulders, all the way through the fingertips, at either sides of the body. The bend is from the waist as hands grip around ankles and the top of the head slowly aims for the floor. Full expression of the posture requires the lower back to arch, sit bones flexed to the sky.

Dandayamana, part of the Sanskrit name for the posture, is what Jaka's dad's friends would call 'a spread leg 6:30,' comparing the arms of a clock to a bent-over body position in side profile. As she returned to standing position that day in class, Nina noticed how Patrice was looking at her in the mirror. Ever since then, he has been overly friendly and beamed at her every chance he got. He seemed to be edging closer to asking her out. She thought he was cute, but was not sure if she was interested beyond that.

3

Jaka & Nina – "Beyond"

Frowning, opening mail and sighing repeatedly, Jaka was slumped in the small, shared office when Nina popped in.

"Morning. How you doing today?" Not waiting for a reply, she continued waving her right hand for emphasis. "So. Lady. What went on here last night? I had to make sure the kids were out and evacuate the premises 'fore we burned up in you all's flames of passion!" Nina joked with her typical flair for exaggeration.

"Yeah, whatever. Thought you were headed to the soothing sweat of hot yoga. There was no danger for you to worry about, Nina. Just carry on with your fast self," Jaka retorted defensively.

"I did teach a 7:30 class. You know, on another tip, I really need to get some day classes on my schedule over there. Luckily it doesn't take long to get home. But I tucked Carlos in at almost 11 and he was so groggy this morning. It was a mess getting that child out the door," Jaka nodded, but seemed distracted by the mail.

"And 'no'. I didn't get any last night," Nina declared, returning to the original topic. "Thanks for asking," she added dryly and rolled her eyes.

"Well, that goes without saying. Shouldn't it? Thought you said you were 'fasting' while the seasons changed," Jaka teased, looking up quizzically from the envelope in her hand.

"Okay Jaka, you go on like that. You feeling all sweet from that loving last night, huh? I'll have you know that I did get a hook up text just before yoga, though."

"That's right," Jaka was having fun now. "A text from your mystery lover, lover?" Teasing Nina was helping her shake off the funk that had settled in after the love-making continued back at her place. "Do they even exist, Nina?"

"What?! Of course they do. Lady please, you know when I've had a good sharing session how I strut all up and down this place glowing and shit. You know that's right," Nina resisted the impulse to throw a snap of her fingers in highlight of her claim. She was 100% city girl, growing up in the downtown core near where she currently lived. Nina used to be a big fan of hip hop. Jaka often teased her about her 'video ho' days where there was not a local music video shoot that she was not somehow involved in.

Nina possessed what many would consider to be a very attractive physique and good-looking face. She was voluptuous in her 5'6 frame with breasts a visually-impaired person could sense were two-handers. Her hips held a bottom that was both ample and firm. Jaka often marveled at how she kept her backside so tight. Of course there were the effects of dance training, yoga plus great genes. Her mother was a smaller, more pear-shaped version of Nina, whose seasoned beauty suggested a youth full of admirers. Nina prided herself on being a head-turner, for both women and men. Over the years, she had learned how to work it to her advantage.

By contrast, Jaka was one of those beauties who seemed unaware of how stunning she was. As she aged, she was inclined to wear progressively less make-up. Except when under the lights. She once explained to Nina she felt it unnecessary to continue hiding behind all that paint any longer. Two years ago, she cut off pretty much all of her hair and continued to keep it low. While her dad and his cricket cronies teased her a lot at first, she received more compliments from others than when she wore braids.

"I know you don't have any problems in the love sharing department, my friend."

"You know that's right," Nina repeated with a dramatic, defiant dip of her head. "Might even have a little rendezvous this weekend, too. And a cute yoga student was trying to talk to me after class yesterday."

"Interesting." Jaka looked up from the papers on the desk in front of her. "You interested? They were in your class?"

"Well, not yesterday. He was outside the studio when I was leaving."

"Ummm...creepy-ish."

"No, come on now. It wasn't like that. He worked late and couldn't make it to the 7:30 class. I just happened to see him across the street when I was leaving. No thing."

"Okay. If you say so. One question though, Nina. Who saw who first?"

Exasperated by her suggestion, she shot Jaka a look that said, 'you are such a carpet-muncher right now you would not begin to understand'.

"Yeah, twist up your face all you want," Jaka said in response to Nina's telling look. "I haven't been with Tashi long enough to forget what it's like to deal with dudes. Just watch for creepy is all."

"Whatever, Jaka. Don't hate on us happily singles."

"Plus he's a client, a student? Okay. Not very professional. That's all I'm saying about that," Jaka added. "On another note, I know you think you smooth with how you describe your little escapades. I've noticed that when you say 'he', you mean 'he'. So when you say 'they', especially when you are so extra about it, it's obvious you are talking about a woman. You see how I worked that clue, right?"

"Don't even bother, detective. It's all good with me. By the way, why aren't you glowing and strutting this fine morning? I know, heard…damn near saw that shared sweetness last night. So why are you sour this morning?" By this point, Nina had plunked herself on the exercise ball by the desk and was balancing upright while stretching out her lower back by concaving her spine.

"Oh Nina, I really don't want to talk about it…but I do. Ugh, where to start?" Jaka sighed sadness as her eyes trailed out the window overlooking the busy street below. "I'm feeling super overwhelmed by things right now. T is terrific, but the pressure and the guilt is getting to me. On top of that things here are messed up – all these damn bills," she shook the mail in her hand in the air as if pleading with the heavens.

"Shrinking class enrollment and disappointing ticket sales at last season's show were hard enough…now we get this letter that the building is being put up for sale in a minimum of six months. Such bullshit! I talked to that fucking George a couple of weeks ago and the bastard said nothing. This means rent will go up or we will be forced to move. Or both! It's not looking or feeling good right now, Nina."

Nina felt for her friend. Even though Jaka was supposedly from the 'hood' and grew up without a mother, she was not particularly street smart. Stress was not her friend. If this situation had happened years ago, Jaka would probably be in one of the studios thrashing out a high-energy, new work with music turned way up. She was great at expressing with her body, words were a struggle. In fact, Nina marveled at how much more verbal Jaka had become since knowing Tashi. It could not have been easy for Tashi at all, Nina smiled to herself recalling the time Jaka spent over four hours working out her stuff in studio. She did not eat or even go to the bathroom. That happened the day she admitted to her father that she was in love with a woman. Needless to say, he flipped out. Then he called Michael.

"So, a night of great sex and you wake to the reality of these money pressures, huh?" Jaka just stared at Nina and sighed again to keep from crying. Nina went on, "Of course this is hard, lady. Just know that I'm right here with you and we will figure this out. Okay? Yes, the building sale is a bit of a surprise. But we knew something was coming. The entire neighbourhood is changing around us!" Nina was right. Waves of gentrification had washed away family-run businesses and low-cost housing for working families. Banks, coffee franchises, high-end restaurants and condos had sprouted up in their place. Tashi was part of a local residents group organizing to ensure affordable housing and needed services remained an integral part of the evolving community.

"Yeah," Jaka agreed and exhaled deeply.

"Lady, I've known you too long and I love you too much to see you so down. You know you have a lot going for you…" Before Nina could finish, Jaka blurted out, "Tashi and I had an argument last night after our sweet time together. Can you believe that shit?"

"Oh no, I'm sorry to hear. What happened?"

"Honestly, Nina. I don't even know. We decided to go back to my place because it's closer. We wanted to extend our enjoyment, shall we say. It was intimate, and freaky, that woman is so…generous," a reminiscent smile came over Jaka's lips. She shook her head. "Then the next thing I know, I'm yelling things I don't mean and she's grabbing her stuff as she bolts out the door!"

"For real?"

"For real, my friend. So strange. After cuddling for a bit she went to the bathroom. I started to doze off waiting for her to flush so that I could go in. A few minutes later, I wake up to Tashi all cold and demanding. She's repeating, 'I said, where is my toothbrush?' I'm a bit groggy and parched, so I look around for the glass of water I'd put by the bed."

"Right." Nina encouraged her friend to continue.

"She snatches up the glass before I could and holds it out of my reach. Can you believe that? Now, I'm awake. I sit up with the most confused, stupid look on my face. I don't even wanna say anything yet cause I'm pissed at her tone and I need some water. <u>And</u> I was just out like a light after hours of awesomeness with said love. Okay? Okay." Nina could tell that Jaka was getting warmed up firing sentiments she felt she could not say last night. "So she says it again, 'Jaka, I'ma ask you one more time. Where is my toothbrush? I was here on Sunday night and my toothbrush was here. I used it. Where is it now? Where it is, Jaka?' Nina, as calmly as I could, and you know how much I hate being woken up like that, I said 'Babes, it should be there. If not, there are some extras. Maybe Dad threw it out. I don't see why you are so upset?'"

"Then she says sarcastically, 'Oh really?'" Jaka continued, "And she is still holding the water like she wants to dash it on me! So Nina, the long and short of it is that she was upset about her toothbrush and used that to pick a fight about moving in together! After we'd had such an amazing time. Just too much!"

"Wonder if she thinks you are cheating and your other lover threw away her toothbrush. Did she check your underwear drawer to see if a next woman's panties were in there?" Nina could not resist poking a little fun.

"Not funny, Nina. I'm not you," Jaka replied dryly. "I can't believe she used that to talk about moving in. And when I said as much she slammed down the glass, got her stuff and stormed out. You know what, though? I really do not need to be stressing about her right now. Not with everything else that's going on around here. You know I love the woman, but come on."

Nina shook her head, "Really, J? For a moment, just take it in from her perspective…if you possibly can." Nina tried to be patient because she knew Jaka could be a bit self-absorbed at times, and miss the obvious as a result. "She probably felt really close to you after all that loving, Jaka. And the toothbrush thing was just a thing. Maybe for her it was a reminder or trigger of some of her insecurities regarding you, your relationship. It's been almost three lezzie years. I've told you this. In the straight world that's like," Nina pretended she was calculating with her fingers. "Carry the three and add…lady, that's like seventeen years in straight people time." Nina giggled. "In her mind, if you really loved her you two would be living together already."

"Excuse me, please. What do you know about the lezzie world? Of adults, I might add. Wanton, random college-girl munching to get back at mommy and daddy is not the same thing."

"Oh really?" Nina quickly retorted. "I know way more than you evidently." She certainly had a lot more experience dealing with women than Jaka did. That was not a challenge since Tashi was only the second woman Jaka had ever seriously dated. "Listen to me, friend from time. She felt hurt and you could have had a more gentle response."

"She caught me off guard. And honestly, I don't need any late-night, out-the-blue relationship drama. She knows that!"

"Wow, J. You aren't the only one going through it, you know. Everybody's got their issues. Don't you think she has pressures, too? How about me? It's all about how you respond. You know that."

"Yeah. I guess."

"Hell, yeah. Consider this situation differently because the glass really is half full. You share in the love of a wonderful person who…"

"'Share in the love'? So sappy, Nina."

"Whatever. Tashi loves you dearly and I've seen you benefit from having her in your life. Besides you could save a lot of money if you shared a place…along with all that love." Nina bounced up, leaned over the desk and kissed her friend on the cheek. "I want the best for you, lady. Think creatively to solve your problems."

"K," Jaka said pouting. "I thought I did but…I kinda see what you mean. From her perspective and all."

"Then my work here is done for now. Carry on." Nina said stepping to the door. She knew she had said enough, and that Jaka needed time to take it in.

"I'm afraid moving in will mess things up." Jaka confessed sadly. Nina turned to face her. "It might make her happy now and solve this relationship hurdle, but we might lose everything down the road. Maybe we'd have no relationship at all. I vowed after Michael…"

"Oh sweet Jesus, lady. Listen to yourself! Michael was a long, long time ago. And he never loved you as much as Tashi does. He just couldn't. You are so blessed, but it's like you don't even know it. Many people would be happy for Tashi's love. Hell, for any part of her. You think seriously about that."

"Yeah, I guess. But look who's talking Miss 'I'm still in love with my ex who dumped me while I was pregnant'. Isn't that calling the kettle black?"

"Ouch, Jaka. Play fair. I can say this to you because I'm letting go of my past, too."

"Seriously…thanks for your wise words, Nina. There's a lot to think about."

"Yes. Including the offer to choreograph and perform a duet at the Denises' wedding."

"Of course. The way things are going looks like we can't turn it down…imagine that bullshit?! Okay, enough of feeling sorry for myself, as you would say. What's on for today?"

4

Sean - "Ready for the Weekend"

Wiped from a long day of rubbing bodies and chatting with clients, Sean dropped her keys on the small table in the dimly-lit hallway and locked the door behind her. Riding her bicycle home in Friday afternoon rush hour traffic had been particularly harrowing. Twice she was almost 'doored' as she sped by parked cars with passengers eager to arrive at their destinations. Thank goodness she had let go of most of the week's stress with her midday work out.

She removed her riding gloves and helmet, resting them next to her keys. As she walked into the bright living room and sunk into the soft, white leather couch, Sean was grateful for all her blessings, big and small. She was grateful for getting home safely, having two jobs she did not hate, it being Friday and choosing this great west-facing apartment so she could enjoy the sunset. She stretched out her legs and nestled into calm. 'Life is good right now,' she thought to herself. 'I've got most of the weekend off and about three hours before linking with the luscious Lindsay and soaking in some live music by the harbour.' She was excited about her plans for the evening, even though none of her friends knew about the rendezvouses she and Lindsay had been enjoying for the past two months.

It was none of their business as far as Sean was concerned. After all, it was not like they were dating. They were just friends with common interests – sports, live music, good food, film festivals. If sex were part of the package, then it would make sense to let her crew know a little about it. But there had been no sex. Despite the crazy sensual energy between them. Not even a kiss. As far as she knew Lindsay preferred men and Sean was not about to press. Lindsay moved through the world as a straight woman. She had a steady boyfriend up until recently. This dynamic was very different than what Sean was used to. Admittedly, it intrigued her a little.

Most of the women she spent time with loved the ladies, and loved off Sean. She preferred it that way. "Why work so hard?" she would often say to her friends with a shoulder shrug and a twist of her lips. "Let them come to you, a wise man once told me. Then let them go. In some cases, hope they go," she would joke.

Playing junior tennis in her teens convinced Sean that she was going to the pros. Most of her peers were convinced, too. In high school and in her neighbourhood, guys and girls alike considered her a boss. Partly because she excelled at an elite sport, one that the sexy Serena and Venus Williams dominated for many years. Partly because she carried herself confidently and exuded genuine warmth in her exchanges with people. Even her fans. Folks felt they knew who she was. Plus she was gorgeous by any measure. High cheek-boned, dimpled with honey-brown smoothness and full, sun-kissed lips, Sean was a definitive girl magnet.

From the outside she seemed like the typical, gay girl. A pretty, soft stud athlete who stretched to 5'7 (press material listed her as 5'8 and a half). She knew everybody and rocked only the latest gear – shoes, watches, clothes, tattoos – on and off the court. Her walk, restless eyes, cocky grin and reputation for being surrounded by beauty, made her a person to watch out for. By being cool with people and appearing assured, yet humble while not smiling too much, Sean remained a mystery. She was considered an attractive, relatively successful enigma, particularly in the queer community. Always with a hot woman or many, depending on the situation, folks were drawn to Sean even though they did not always know what to make of her. The lovers that were closest to her over the years, were the ones who stuck around despite, or because, of her fun-first, 'work smart, play smarter' reputation.

She enjoyed her status and worked hard to keep her name clean. Sean much preferred to keep her freakiness under wraps. She liked partying at friend's places and hotels instead of clubs, delighted in porn and strippers instead of sex parties. Folks would see her out, sometimes with her crew, sometimes with the ladies. But she prided herself on no drama, no 'reality show type' stunts in her social life. People could not point a finger or flash a video and say anything really negative about her regarding the freak factor. In public, Sean was a gracious gentlewoman.

Inside, behind closed doors, she made time to explore herself and others. She treasured talented strippers, good porn and a self-respecting freak. Preferably all in the same night. Especially if dark-skin, big asses, real titties and hair-you-can-hold-onto were involved.

This had been a tough week because Sean somehow managed to not hook up with any of her three friends with benefits. Despite best efforts, including a few semi-desperate texts, schedules could not synch up. Between her massage and tennis lesson clients, she had booked over forty-seven billable hours that week. She was exhausted, horny and excited about the evening ahead. One hundred percent heterosexual or not, Lindsay was a dime when Sean factored in her boundless intellect and solid frame that seemed capable of so many things. But she resisted her natural urge to step to her. Too stereotypical for the lezzie to hit on the straight woman. Sean felt that Lindsay knew what was up and that she would put it out there if, and when, she was ready.

As part of her no-drama approach to loving, Sean preferred when things were clear.

Like the time she woke up at a buddy's hotel party fully clothed with a pantied pussy pasted on her face. Or when ever a woman rubs up against her as they are entering Sean's condo, the 'Pleasure Palace' as her friends jokingly called it.

Sean had this thing where she would not bring women to her place for weeks. Anticipation and curiousity would build in this time. They would wonder, 'Does she live in a hole? Is her woman up in there? Why doesn't she want me to come over?' Then their musings might escalate to, 'What's she got up in there anyway? Ima reach up in that spot!' The entire time Sean would be down-playing her place. Listening sensitively to questions, complaints, hints, accusations and side-eyes about whatever. This tactic often showed Sean a lot about a women's character. A tactic transferred from the tennis court. Growing up, she always remembered her grandmother advising, "De higher monkey climb, de more he does show he tail."

Sean made time for her freaky sex and her porn. Yet she also felt confident she could always get pussy. While she liked to think that this was a result of her charming personality and warm soul, it was probably more because of her looks and the perception that she was balling. Sean realized long ago that people were going to think what they were going to think, positive or negative. So instead of focusing on changing minds, she zoned in on understanding their approach, then using it to her advantage. Just like in tennis. With opponents and with the ladies, she researched their game and adapted hers to suit. Were they aggressive? Hitting hard balls, blasting serves, seeking to intimidate? Or were they under the radar? Holding back a bit to see your game while letting you underestimate them? Maybe they just shook you initially leaving you not quite sure what to expect. Regardless of the play, Sean usually had an effective response. She was proud of how she translated her court skills especially since she had discovered the hard way that, for some, love was a sport.

As much as Sean like to get down, she did not respond to anything that was too vague or open to misinterpretation. She stuck with situations, and people, she knew and could trust. If all else failed, there was always her vast and ever-evolving porn collection. As a gay athlete, and especially since she was growing her massage practice, Sean could not afford to have a reputation as an ass-hungry, skirt chaser. 'Hell, no! Not Erlene Jordan's daughter,' she thought to herself. Her momma may still not approve of her out lesbianess ("Why you can't just hush your mouth and dress like a girl, Seanitah?!"), but she certainly would not stand for Sean being known as desperate and needing to chase down love.

She always knew her momma struggled to tolerate her 'lifestyle' even though she loved her only daughter the best she could. Sean found out the limits of her momma's love during a crisis. During her first, and only, heartbreak she was away at school and had sustained a career-altering shoulder injury during a tournament in Miami. Her momma flew to her side to ensure her body healed, but wanted to hear nothing of her crushed heart. The most her momma could muster was an angry, "Good, glad! Dat blasted gal can carry on with her nasty, dutty lifestyle. Leave my daughter alone."

Sean shook her head, 'Damn, why am I thinking about all this mess right now? I wanna get in my cool, sexy zone.' She got up and poured herself a dark rum with lime over ice. As she sipped the strong drink she liberated a half-smoked joint from her stash box, then returned to the couch. After a couple of pulls, Sean picked up the remote. She let her shoulders drop, knees fall apart. She relaxed into herself. Yet there was tension that needed her attention. She had not had sex since Saturday night and was not about to hang with Lindsay feeling any kind of horny. That would be a recipe for disaster. Then for sure Sean would say or do something stupid out of sheer horniness. She called up an engaging video, one she had been saving for a special occasion, and enjoyed sweet release before the opening sequence had finished.

As Sean savoured her own afterglow, Derek, one of her drinking buddies called. She decided to answer.

"Hey you," he started after they exchanged greetings. "Don't forget I'm spinning at The Drop tonight. No cover, so come through and bring a friend. Or two."

"I just might. Here chilling right now. About to head out inna couple."

"What you up to?"

"There's a live cumbia band at the harbor from 9 to 11. Checking it out with a friend."

"Nice. Friend, huh? Sounds like a date to me."

"It's not a date."

"Watch out now, tiger. Sure she knows that?"

"Bye, Derek."

"See you later, right?"

"Probably. Have a great set!"

She pressed end on the phone and play on the remote. As she was having a second look, it occurred to her that the short, lean-bodied actor with the long, light-brown lace front weave reminded her a little of Shy One. Sean admired a bad bitch who wanted to show her how much 'badder' she was than the next girl. And there was nothing better than when a few of them wanted to show who was 'baddest'.

Last year during her birthday weekend, Sean enjoyed the company of three stunning hotties of different ethnicities, body types and sexual strengths. Midway through the night, not even trying to mess up their names (in case she wanted to spend quality time with them again), Sean started referring to them as Nasty One, Shy One and Champion. They played along with it. Claiming their monikers, each tried to outdo one another in what turned into a fabulous role play. For a while, it was like Sean was not even there. They were so into the hotness competition, she just sat back and watched. Live private porn right in front of her eyes. The sexy kind that compels you reach out, touch and give instructions. That was the kind of living that Sean was about.

Two of the women were ones that she had been with before. The third was someone Derek had introduced her to that evening. All were freaks and, over the course of the night, Sean realized that they all seemed to know one another. From the way they handled themselves, it was quite likely that these three had been in similar situations in the past. She did not care. But she did cum over and over again for hours. It was her birthday. Sean made every one of them feel celebrated until she, and they, were exhausted. It was one of the best sexual experiences of her life. The last thing she remembered was slipping off to sleep after cumming for the 100th time. She had three fingers on each hand plunged into Shy One and Nasty One respectively...and respectfully.

When Sean woke up, she found Shy One perusing her porn collection, Nasty One sipping a latte and ordering room service. Champion was pouring a tequila shot while pulling on her knee-high stiletto boots. Watching the Friday-evening sunset and recalling the pleasure of all three lovelies out-doing each other in sucking her off, Sean stroked her special spot in that special way and came for a second time.

'Best night ever for the unparalleled freak factor,' Sean thought as her breathing slowed to normal. But on her list of friends who could get it, Lindsay was at the top. Sean had a sense that Lindsay might want to share something with her tonight. Either way, she was determined to work Derek's 'principle of least interest'. With her game face on, Lindsay would not be able to tell if she was feeling aroused or not. Even if they ended up randomly brushing against one another during a dance or if Lindsay "accidentally" bounced up on Sean's crotch like she did last time they were out. Unlike a dude, Sean's hardness (and wetness) for Lindsay would be concealed. She would have to be determined to dig down and explore.

As an accomplished professional, and one of the few women of colour in her field, Lindsay was used to drawing attention. Men and women alike noticed her because she resembled a short, thick version of a runway model and sounded like Michelle Obama ("the FLOTUS"). That was not a coincidence because she idolized Michelle. She had been called to the bar by twenty-two and, after articling at a top taxation firm, was about to make partner less than 10 years later. She also taught a class on corporate taxation law at one of the local universities. Hair, face, nails always done, Lindsay personified the 'lady in the street' adage.

After years of loving women, dozens and dozens since her first encounter with a tennis buddy at fourteen, Sean could smell a freak a mile away. She knew Lindsay was the type who, because of her busy career, probably did not have much time for sex. Sean guessed that given how important efficiency was to her, when she did make the time she wanted it, needed it to be the 'hanging from the chandelier' variety. Because who knew when it would happen again.

Sean wondered what Lindsay was going to wear that night. While calling up mental pictures of low-cut necklines and body-kissing waistlines, she remembered that focusing her sexual energy on Lindsay was the opposite of what she was trying to do. The video and the flashback had been great to burn off some steam, but she figured a third orgasm for good measure could not hurt. Then she would shower, feel reinvigorated and be out the door.

This time she decided to recreate the best parts of her most recent sexual encounter in her mind. Her on-again, off-again lover Pat, an attractive, recently-divorced mother of two teens, was going to star in this scene. One of the things Sean liked most about Pat was that she could take it for hours. As a result, their sex sessions were marathon. Their loving often took so much time, required so much recovery and was so loud, the two could only link on weekends when the kids were at their father's. If they managed to get in two marathons a month they were lucky. On Saturday, Pat had put it on her like syrup on pancakes. She did every time. Sean pressed herself into the softness of the seat beneath and reminisced with a smirk. Eyes closed, she slid her hands further in between her thighs. She envisioned being engulfed by tight, quivering flesh. Warm lips relished over her responsive clit.

"Ahhh," she moaned moments later as the sun said goodbye to the day. "Now, I'm ready for the weekend."

Tashi's Poems

want love you

want you
to make *ifa* with me
slow & rough, gentle & probing
ever/feeling the tempo
we will go to the edge
over
& back again with care & passion

want to feel you in my hair
dreading
yet anticipating the seasons of our coming
together
want you to seep beneath the skin
unlodge yourself
& slip deep into my flesh

want to extend past mind/fuck
intellectualizing with some hands-on
expression
want you to lay your lips on me
demanding I sip sweetly from your familiar
temple 'til this never/ending ritual
strokes divinities only imaged

yessss
want you
to want to open up
using no tongues other than the languages we
share

want the miracle of this union
to re/trace depths of lives past

want us to be left wet
slippery with the energy of our spent
imaginations
yet still full of piqued curiousity

in this moment

in this movement
of slow whining passion
bodies dance praises
honouring higher forces
and minds mesh
with mutual in/securities

cautious kisses
cloud
soul/full desire
as we swallow
fluid mind body response
and lick wounds of in/visibility

in this moment
endless as forever
full as the moon
we ascend to love
over/climbing stars
marking our paths
        with fleeting certainty

in this moment
past present pain
continues to haunt
and the twilight sky/scape offers little
comfort...
dusk/rinsed vulnerability
burns still sensitive eyes
and dries our throats
to communication

in this moment
of personal politics
and
self/created identities
difference
is opportunity for deeper understanding

i love you
in this moment

Play Me

i.
synch your downstroke into me
groove my dissonant ass
just the way you like it
bend my back
nipples bopping
fingers finding
skin circling
slippery sweet

come
play me
drum in tempo
hard on
head first
into raw resonance

ii.
reverb my soul
rock us steady
rhythm snapping
mouth open
pussy popping

to your beat
me
into sublime submission

'take it cuz you know it's yours
that's the way
uh huh
uh huh'

iii.
riding your horn
you orchestrate me
sweet
neck
back
hips
legs
up
ready
open
for your pulsating pitch
moist melodies
churn chords
to climatic crescendo

only you with
your soulful bass lovingness
could play me like this

unexpectedly exciting (for Jaka)

your spirit moves me
to passionate, insightful emotion
w/ words, eyes, ideas, hips, quips, lips...
a sacred whisper in time
shared
sweetly
surprisingly

your lips on mine
speaking volumes
ecstatic
our souls stretch to reach
in gentle, firm embrace

pulling me close w/ sultry subtly
you incite me
to dance with images
to think boundlessly
to feel your essence

thank you for pressing your sweetness
up against mine
confirming we complement
in a kismet kiss

know that i absolutely adore you
w/ awe & admiration
my universe is forever changed now
that you are in it

toward continued revelation & luscious
lovemaking…

untitled

your refusal
swims in the air of my desire

caught
suspended under
currents of repeated dreams
hoping to lose themselves
in self-protective analysis

surfacing again
fear grows down
deepening wells of beauty
rooting unspoken kisses

watchful ears
unearth calm waves
washing forth clarity
sucks
at my confusion
and half answered questions
continue to resist

Used To Be

Used to be
Pending cold froze my gratitude
For fall's orangeredyellowgreen browness

Used to be
Your love scared me
You'd hold me tight,
Read my soul and
Make me wanna flee

Used to be
I couldn't see the forest
For the trees

Used to be
Your love couldn't be real
How could it be? So suddenly?
When you don't' even know me?

Used to be…no
Used to feel
You'd disappear

That I would slip away
In the dark of day

But now
My warmth radiates internally
Eternally savouring each season

But now
It's about how I FEEL with you
And how your arms remain wrapped around me
Even after you leave

But now
The realness of us flows
And grows
Cuz I got me and you got you
Like never before

Now
We chose faith
With fearless hearts
In pursuit of passion
We blossom with abandon
Love free
Being ALL of we
You and me

Recalibrate

things fallen apart
like
water-soaked metal

rusted
mental machinations
automate silence
no steady hum of breath
instead
elements exposed
like cracked pipes
seeping the unseen

apart at the seams
volume-busting pressure
bubbling
from the core
breaks parts into parts
that don't fit no more

now
screws loose
joints grind

spokes spike &
bolts unwind

you in your semi-solid state
me in mine

...system reset
settle and rewind
recalibrate

refresh air/tight
e-powered possibilities
for optimal performance
&
smooth sliding parts
around parts that
align synchronized
regenerating
energized
blended balance
once more

let's recalibrate
& explore what's in store

on coming

"be not conformed to this world, but be
transformed by the renewal of your minds"
                              romans 12:2

on coming
out
from deceptive denial
and painful pasts
we, creator's chosen,
transcend confusion
expand the reality of difference…
mind/full of freedom
and ascendant love

on coming
into
the stillness of self
and spiritual sustenance
we
abandon acceptance
embrace exposure
risking solace…rejection?
seeking truth…transformation

on coming
through
moans of forever
and supple suggestion
we, creator's chosen,
eclipse ecstasy
overcome oppression
become
fresh
faith full
fear free

revolutionary sounds

she came
crashing into me
like many militant raindrops

beads of de/fi/ance
glistened so sweet
on her diva face
etching a silent path
      to be followed

"wade in the water"

cautious still
I lean in to wipe her wet brow
& hear the echo of ebon cries...
uhuru & msago
resonate resistance
drummed up deep
from her soul

rain/claps amplify
chanting in song

in speech
in deliverance of voices
everywhere
she came
locks flying like my mama's lash
to un/en/tangle my mind
noisy with dissonance and nearly hit notes

she came
swaying to her own rhythmic zami/vibes
catching ancestral spirits
of syncopated silence

contracting chords of rage reverberate
& ring my battle/bell
for liberation

she came
full/conscious
with her lyrical self
& grooved me to the ancient vibrations of
revolutionary sounds

this lesbian poem

this lesbian poem
is for all those sistas
who wonder what 2 women do
& for all those who know
the endless possibilities

this lesbian poem
takes her place as *part of the family*
she is a
stud/femme/stem/andro/trans
single/involved/married/open/
monogamous/just curious
and respectful of the many ways we be
kind of poem

one
this lesbian poem
is a dyke of the cosmos
but she ain't no alternative advertising
trick

she isn't fooled
by propped up media pseudo-lesbo hype
posing vague, trendy couplings of
sister   daughter/mother   friends   ???
this lesbian poem
being loving women
since before it was
h o t
she a 24/7 dyke
whose gonna take her 15 minutes
of fleeting flame
& keep on steppin'

two
this lesbian poem
is for the sistas who try
to wash their pain
with the blood of others...
tired
of the popular power games,
insecurities, fear & past horror
turned nasty
acting out & scarring deep

this lesbian poem
will <u>not</u> kick you in the gut
sex you against your will
slap you across the room or
call you an ugly, worthless piece of shit
no
this lesbian poem
will dance to the beat of your clit
fuck you sweet
without force
in this violent world
as she struggles to love
herself
& you

three
resisting the dirt and disrespect
of internalized hate...
this lesbian poem
is OUT in the life
maturing with the responsibility
of her personal power

this lesbian poem
joins the flow
of pieces by pussy-sucking sistas
everywhere
testifyin' 'bout our movements,
sanctifyin' our unions
solidifyin' our resistance

as dawns cracks
this mutha/cunt
will express her sexuality
wide open & in colour
even after she is born again

About the Author

Akhaji Zakiya is a writer, educator and producer. Her work has been published in "The Great Black North - Contemporary African Canadian Poetry" and "Does Your Mama Know? - An Anthology of Black Lesbian Coming Out Stories". She lives in Toronto with roots that extend from West Africa to the Caribbean. This is her first collection of writing. Look out for her first novel in fall of 2015.